MANOR FARM

Sandra Tyson

To Martin and Rebecca

ISBN 978-1-8382128-1-0

Cover design by: Danni Henning

Publisher – Ernstoff and Tyson Publishing

One

It was election time on Manor Farm. As always, emotions ran high with opinions strongly divided on who would make the best leader.

Many years ago, when the humans were expelled, the animals had such faith in Napoleon that they did not need elections. But life had proved to be harder and more complicated than anyone had expected, both economically and politically.

To increase production for the benefit of all, the Farm was divided into individual plots, which were privately owned by those animals (mostly pigs) who were deemed capable. In return, they had to give up a share of their crops in taxes for distribution to those in need.

After Napoleon's death, there was a farm wide debate about the future. A new system of government was set up that everyone agreed was the best way to run the Farm.

At the top sat the President, who had to be either a pig or a dog because they were the cleverest. Two Barns, one of Pigs and the other of Dogs, set the laws. And a Parliament of wise owls was responsible for interpreting and applying them.

The President and Barns were elected democratically – one animal, one vote. The owls were appointed by the President. The system worked well.

This election was particularly controversial. The outgoing President, Nelson, was the first black retriever to be elected to such an exalted position. He had raised rations for retired animals, promoted organic farming, built a hospital and brought in improvements to increase productivity and prosperity. But the traditionally minded pigs attacked and obstructed everything he tried to do. The most extreme claimed he had not been born on the Farm, which they knew was untrue. He was too intelligent and principled to respond. Most of the animals loved and respected him, but he was opposed by the sheep who always obeyed the pigs, the pigeons and the most fervent believers in the Sugar Candy Mountain.

It was time for him to hand over to a successor. The two candidates were Mickey, an elderly and somewhat overweight white pig, and Jess, a female dog. The campaign was bitter and dirty.

Mickey had inherited great riches from his father. He used his wealth to fund numerous schemes and businesses, most of which failed, but mysteriously he never seemed to get any poorer. He and his pretty but empty headed wife Minnie had been in the forefront of the 'birther' conspiracy against Nelson, which was strange because she was born and brought up on Soy

Farm. And, even more oddly, those animals who were usually the most hostile to settlers from other farms never criticised her.

Jess's husband had been President back in the day. Able and experienced, she was the obvious frontrunner, but her prospects were harmed by Farm gossip - that she was only a candidate because of her husband and that Presidents should be pigs or dogs, not sows or bitches.

Jess campaigned on the issues. Building on Nelson's legacy, she promised to develop constructive relationships with humans and neighbouring farms, increase productivity and share the proceeds fairly, train young animals for work and give those who had worked hard a comfortable retirement.

But she struggled to get her message across in the face of attacks from Mickey and his followers. He accused her of sharing confidential information with other farms. At campaign meetings, he whipped up crowds with cries of 'She's a traitor. Lock her up!'

'Lock her up' bleated the sheep.

The pigeons flew around the Farm tweeting 'Lock her up. Lock her up.' They repeated it so often and so loudly that, despite Jess's impressive policies and considered arguments, many animals wondered whether she had done anything wrong. And, just in case anyone had missed the tweets, the rumours and accusations were reported all day every day on the popular radio station, Rat News.

Election campaigns had always been civil and constructive. This was war.

Two

On a cool evening, after a long day's work, three friends were relaxing at the North East Trough, drinking water and looking out over the fields and meadows of their beloved farm. Clara was a clever donkey, Diego a llama from neighbouring Pinto Farm and Bella a loyal and friendly cow. Conversation inevitably turned to the election. It was all anyone was talking about.

'Mickey's promised to stand up for the Farm. That's what we need – to make the farm great again.' Bella was such a devotee she was wearing a hat with MMGA – Make Manor Great Again – his official slogan.

'Huh' brayed Clara, who was not an easy beast to convince. 'He's just playing on animals' fears. He doesn't have the first idea how to do anything.'

'Of course he does' Bella replied. 'He's a very successful business pig. That's why he's so rich.'

'No. He got his money from his father. Most of his businesses have been failures.'

They were both right. He had indeed inherited huge wealth and he had started many businesses. A few had been very profitable –

the Mickey Hotel Barn, a golf course on land close to the farm and a herd of alpacas whose fleeces were sought after by humans. But there were many short lived ventures too – Mickey vodka made from corn and Mickey College which ran largely useless training courses. Whether he had made money or not was unclear, not least because he refused to release information on his finances.

'Anyway' said Bella, trying to move onto safer ground. 'He'll look after us. He'll fight corruption. And stop Mung Farm selling its products too cheaply. He's going to build a wall to stop animals coming here illegally from Pinto Farm. He'll close Nelson's hospital to stop wasting money.' She smiled, happy at the thought of all the good this would do. 'And he's going to drain the swamp.' The swamp was riddled with mosquitoes, a species hated by everyone on the Farm, and it would make a good meadow for grazing cows.

Clara shook her head. 'All nonsense. He's more corrupt than the animals he's criticising. If we don't have a hospital, we won't have proper health care. Where will the frogs live if there's no swamp? As for Mung Farm, trade helps everyone. And we need animals from other farms to work here.' She turned to Diego. 'You come from Pinto. You can't possibly support him.'

Diego blushed. 'I do think Mickey will be best for us all. And I agree with him. The Farm needs workers, but too many animals won't do their bit. Even some immigrants.'

'Funny how they're blamed for taking jobs from native farm animals and at the same time of being lazy and refusing to work' Clara pointed out. 'I fear for this farm if that pig wins. Look at how he treats his wife. No respect at all. And you must have heard the stories about how he behaves with all females.' Rumours about his activities with the youngest and prettiest alpacas were rife.

But Bella and Diego were not convinced. It was hard to persuade animals who got most of their information from Rat News and pigeon tweets. Clara hoped enough voters would understand. She knew Jess would make a great President and the thought of Mickey was more than she could bear.

Three

Mickey was known for making deals. He called his talent as a business pig 'the art of the squeal'. But he had never shown any interest in politics. Surprisingly, although he was quick to attack Jess and the dogs, he was easily upset by criticism.   And his lack of knowledge about policies and governance was exposed by Jess, who had served with honour under President Nelson. Everyone expected her to win.

When the results were announced, it was a shock to almost every animal on the Farm. Mickey had won. He would be the new President. The sheep were so delighted they went to the Jess strongholds to bleat Mickey's name. The pigeons tweeted away 'Make Manor Farm Great Again. Manor First. Lock Her Up. And Build That Wall.'

The inauguration ceremony was a hugely important occasion. Mickey was dressed formally, his bulky chest puffed out and his expression serious. He held up his right trotter, stumbling slightly over the oath "I do solemnly swear that I will faithfully execute the Office of President of Manor Farm and will to the best of my ability, preserve, protect and defend the legacy of Major." Major was the wise old pig whose dream had started the rebellion against the humans. He was buried in the orchard and his statue stood outside the President's home, the White Barn.

CNN (the Creature News Network) reported that Minnie cried when the results were announced, a story her husband condemned as 'fake news'. But her stony face suggested she was not looking forward to life as First Sow.

Mickey did not look happy either. He had achieved what he had set out to do; he was the most important animal on the Farm. But he still hated his predecessor, resentful of his continuing popularity and furious to see a crowd so much smaller than the one at Nelson's inauguration. The sheep were out in force and the pigeons too, when they were not flying around the Farm tweeting at the other animals to attend. The ravens brought their disciples, convinced that Mickey's leadership would take them a step closer to the Sugar Candy Mountain. Many small animals were there, but they took up little space. The turnout of the other animals was poor -- dogs, goats, chickens, cows and donkeys. The cats were nowhere to be seen, offended at reports that Mickey said he liked to 'grab pussy'. The llamas were split; some hated him because of his hostility to immigrants while others supported him because they were already living on the Farm. Diego was confused by Rat News reports of attendance higher than at Nelson's inauguration. 'The meadow looked empty from where I was standing. I must have got it wrong.'

Despite her disappointment, Clara did not panic when Mickey took office. Before elections, politicians said what they thought the voters wanted to hear, but they often broke their promises. To her horror, it turned out he meant exactly what he said. His hostility to Pinto Farm continued after he took office. He asked the Barns of Pigs and Dogs to release funding for the Wall. The Pigs agreed straight away, but the Dogs refused. Clara explained their reasons to Diego and Bella. 'Firstly, it will cost a lot of money, money that would be better spent on supporting the animals who live here. Secondly, we don't know how to build such a big wall. Thirdly, there are other ways to get here. Animals can climb over or burrow under a Wall. Or they can go round it and come in through other farms. We can't have a wall surrounding the whole Farm. It's ridiculous.'

'But Mickey knows what he's doing. We are being overrun. We need to protect Manor jobs for Manor animals. Manor First.' protested Bella.

'It's lies put out by Mickey and his friends at Rat News' brayed Clara, trying to stay calm, because she knew Bella was a good and decent cow; she had been fooled by Mickey's propaganda. 'Our prosperity depends on bringing in workers who will do the jobs our animals can't or won't do. Settlers give more to the Farm than they take from it. Take Diego here. He works harder than anyone, don't you?'

Diego smiled shyly. 'I try my best.' No one could have been more loyal than Diego. He was so grateful to his new home farm that he resolved to spend an extra half an hour each day pulling, pushing and carrying. He was young, strong, fit and keen to help his fellow animals. He was sure his loyalty would be rewarded. He planned to bring his wife and children over from Pinto Farm to live with him very soon. When he told his friends, Clara smiled, but her eyes were sad.

Four

Mickey struggled to put a team together. Staff came and went. Either he did not trust them to obey his orders or they could not deal with his foibles. He demanded total loyalty. For him, there was no distinction between loyalty to him as an individual pig and as head of the Farm.

Pigs held most senior positions and many of them were related to Mickey. His youngest son, Minnie's child, was still a piglet, rarely seen in public. He had other children from his previous sows, all vociferous champions for their father.

One son, Mortimer, travelled all over the Farm, trying to impress Mickey by delivering his messages in harsher language even than his father: crime and violence would end when the wall stopped immigrants from Pinto Farm and all dogs were enemies of the Farm. He was only listened to because he was Mickey's son.

Clara was a historian. Like her fellow donkeys, she remembered everything and stories of the revolution had been passed down to her by her ancestors. She believed in Major's vision of equality. Now, not only were some animals more equal than others, but some pigs were more equal than others, even if they were as stupid as Mortimer.

The Farm was becoming dangerously divided between the pigs and the dogs, each accusing the other of corruption. The pigs denounced the dogs for being too close to Soy and Mung Farms. Mickey promised to root out corruption, but he only ever spoke of corrupt dogs and the animals that supported them.

Bella was loyal to Mickey but even she found Mortimer's speeches too extreme, especially when they were tweeted over and over again by the pigeons. Some of her best friends were sheep and she felt uneasy when they lapped up his every word, even when he hinted they were dumb.

She preferred to talk about Melody, Mickey's daughter. Her father really loved her. He described her as the most beautiful sow in the world. Those who had met her said she appeared sweet and well mannered, but she believed that rich pigs were better than any other animals and that she was the best of them all. She had little understanding of farming or government and only slightly more of the businesses she supposedly ran herself - fashion and beauty for the wealthiest sows.

Neither child was suited to running the Farm, so it was a shock when they were appointed to key posts in the administration. They often represented their father at meetings. He did not like listening to or debating with others. He claimed to have exceptional instincts for politics, government, science, medicine and law, so he had no need for expert advice. Anyway, written advice was long and boring. Having known him all their lives, his children knew better than to challenge him, so they were ideal advisers.

He spent his days playing games, listening to Rat News, working on his private businesses and campaigning for the next election, because he wanted to be President for as long as he could. He addressed rallies twice a week, continuing to lead chants of 'Lock her up' even though Jess had said little since her defeat and an investigation had exonerated her. And he spoke regularly to the pigeons, feeding them messages to tweet all over the Farm. That was much more to his taste than the real work of government.

Clara snorted 'He's so stupid. He has no idea. He thinks if he shouts, things will change. And he doesn't care about anyone or anything except money.'

Diego thought that was unfair. Like Bella, he still wore his MMGA cap, which protected him from the sun as he worked long hours in the fields. 'Mickey knows about business. He knows we have to stop imports from Mung Farm and the wrong sort of immigrants from Pinto Farm. Then we'll have Farm jobs for Farm animals and there will be more crops and food for all of us.' He had listened hard and he was sure that was right.

Five

Despite the promises and the celebratory tweets, many animals felt they were becoming poorer. Even Bella suspected rations were getting smaller. She felt starving long before they arrived each day and, quite often, hungry again shortly after eating. Under their coats, the sheep looked thinner. The goats and chickens complained, but they and the dogs were shouted down by the pigs, the sheep and the pigeons. The pigeons were becoming highly skilled at swooping down and tweeting all together, so it was almost impossible to be heard over the noise.

Senior dogs met secretly when the other animals were asleep. The Barker of the Barn of Dogs was a fiercely intelligent and mature bitch called Lucia. She chaired the first meeting. 'It's good to see so many of you here' she barked. 'We all share the same aim. To save the Farm and get proper government again as soon as possible.'

That was true and no one disagreed. The disputes started when they tackled the difficult questions - what should be done, when, how and by whom. A group of younger dogs, new to the Barn, was particularly vocal, demanding Mickey's immediate removal. They were bright, lively and popular, but barely out of puppyhood.

Older, wiser heads feared their tactics would win battles, but lose the war.

Lucia explained. 'We have to make sure Mickey doesn't win the next election. Getting him out earlier would be a bonus, but make no mistake, he'll fight us all the way. And he still has a strong base. He's not a clever pig, far from it, but he's wily and manipulative. He knows how to appeal to the worst in creatures. We have to be as crafty as he is.'

'No' argued one of the young terriers. 'We have to do what's right. We know rations have been cut. It's Mickey's fault. Everything goes to his friends and family, so there's not enough to go round. We have to educate all the animals so they understand. Life could be so much better if we learn to share and to love each other.'

Lucia did not want to discourage the young pups, who were the future leaders of the dog community, but she could not risk tearing the Farm apart without being certain of destroying Mickey. She said would criticise him, but also negotiate to moderate his policies and to protect the weakest animals from their impact. That would give time for the dogs to unite behind the candidate best placed to beat Mickey at the next election. The youngsters growled their disagreement. They did not yet have the support to challenge the older dog, but, if things continued as they were, they soon would.

The contenders spoke at meetings across the Farm. Each had a different approach. Some wanted to return to the halcyon days when Nelson was in charge. Others believed voters should be offered Mickeyism with the worst excesses removed. The most radical wanted to take over private businesses and to return the land to common ownership. Lucia was worried the dogs might get carried away and support that. It sounded good, but were the proposals achievable and would the voters go for them? The danger was that Mickey and his followers would accuse them of wanting to steal private property from those creating wealth, leading to poverty for all. In her view, radical policies were all very well, but risking defeat was self-indulgent, because another Mickey term of office would harm those most in need.

The meetings were lively, with the candidates and their champions expressing their opinions loudly and passionately. Mickey had his spies there. No one knew who they were, but everyone was sure they were listening, observing and reporting back. After each meeting, the pigeons were out and about tweeting Mickey's attacks on the dogs – accusing them of disloyalty, being in the pay of the Mungs and the Soys and of being unfit to run the Farm. Every problem was blamed on Nelson. Mickey claimed only he could solve them.

Clara attended the meetings and listened carefully to all the speeches. She had no doubt they would all be better than Mickey, but who was the strongest? She thought hard and studied her history to try to work out the answer. Like most donkeys, she had always supported the dogs. In her opinion, Nelson was a brilliant and honourable dog, who had achieved as much as any President could on a Farm that was difficult to run. She agreed with Lucia that Mickey had to be defeated. She hoped for a candidate who would be more than just better than Mickey, a leader who understood the animals' fears and desires, who could communicate with them and who would improve their lives.

Week after week, the animals listened, discussed and considered. Candidates with insufficient votes dropped out. The eventual winner was Jack, an elderly moderate who had worked closely with Nelson. He was not radical enough for some, but he was well liked across the Farm and known to be decent and honourable. The dogs were so fearful of another term for Mickey that even those who had reservations about his candidacy united to support him.

Six

Mickey's rule was proving even more controversial than his fiercest opponents had feared.

His policies were often made on the trotter to garner popularity. But he was committed to his key priorities.

His messages were clear, consistent, simple and difficult to counter. He said rations had increased. Lucia said this was a lie and they had been cut. Reducing contributions from private landowners would, according to Mickey, encourage them to produce more for the benefit of all. Lucia replied that lower contributions would simply make the private owners richer. He sneered at her, calling her Loopy Lucia.

The three friends talked about it. 'Maybe' suggested Diego 'rations are going up, but I feel hungry because I'm working so hard. It's a small price to pay for the good of the whole Farm.'

Clara reminded them that the animals had wanted fair shares for all after the Revolution, but soon afterwards they were faced with more work, lower rations and hoarding by the pigs. 'And now it's getting worse.'

Bella felt torn. Many of her fellow cows were losing faith with Mickey and turning to the dogs as they had done in Nelson's day. She was convinced Mickey was not telling the truth about the rations, but she listened to him to try to understand why. 'If too many immigrants are coming to the Farm, not working hard and expecting to be fed, of course there are shortages. That's why we have to have the Wall.'

Mickey was obsessed with Mung Farm. Everyone knew it was a tough Farm with secretive and dictatorial owners whose animals were tortured and overworked. But Mickey cared about trade, not animal rights. He accepted that selling crops to animals and humans across the country would bring the Farm the income to pay for what it could not produce. But, he contended, trade had to be fair. The Mungs sold their produce too cheaply, so he proposed tariffs on imports.

Lucia, Jack and the dogs argued that would just make things worse. 'Imports will cost more and other farms will retaliate. Exports of our eggs, crops and wool will drop. Everyone will be poorer.'

Mickey kept it simple. 'We're at war with Mung Farm. The dogs are on the side of our enemy.' The pigeons tweeted it all over the Farm. They looked as plump and healthy as ever. The sheep were quieter, but they were thin and weak.

His attitude to Soy Farm was very different. He called its owner, Ivan, a friend. Why, Clara asked herself, would he hate Mung and love Soy? What was so different about the two farms? Both were run by humans. Both treated their animals harshly. Nelson had managed relations with other farms cautiously and judiciously, using trade to benefit all parties and promoting animal rights whenever he could. Mickey had no interest in the wellbeing of his fellow creatures outside Manor Farm. That was what Manor First meant.

He proposed to create more wealth on the Farm by reducing regulation. That sounded sensible. But regulation did not only mean rules, checks and inspections; it also meant safety, standards and expert advice. There were reports of illnesses as controls over the quality of foodstuffs were relaxed and the use of fertilisers increased. Mickey denounced them as lies spread by his opponents.

Diego worked harder and harder, keen to demonstrate his loyalty to the regime so his family would be allowed to join him. And, with regulation reduced, there was no limit to how many hours he could work. He got so tired Clara thought he took longer to achieve less. He refused to discuss it.

Healthcare was a hot topic. Why was Mickey so set on closing the hospital? He denied rumours that he owned a hospital on Soy Farm, blaming his enemies for spreading fake news. Could it really be because he did not want to spend so much on maintaining the animals' health? That would be short sighted, because sick animals were unproductive. He said he had put in place a new and better contract to use other farms' medical care. Rat News reported on how well this was going, but vets were rarely seen on the Farm and only the very sickest animals were taken away for treatment. Most never returned.

Seven

Entering the Farm was getting harder. According to the White Barn spokespig, the proposed 'reforms would advance the safety and prosperity of all animals while helping new citizens to assimilate and flourish.' Although that sounded good, it didn't match Mickey's rhetoric. He condemned recent arrivals, especially those from Pinto Farm, as criminals, thieves and killers.

'There are some very bad animals invading us' he said. 'Go back to where you come from. You won't be admitted to our great Farm unless you have special permission. Our brave police are waiting for you!' This was tweeted again and again by the pigeons and broadcast on Rat News. When he was accused of being hostile to fellow creatures, he said "I don't care about whining from the runts of the dog litter. Everyone else agrees with me."

New settlers were supposed to come through the main gate. Mickey had the gate moved to the far north of the Farm to make it harder to get there from Pinto to the south. So they got in wherever and however they could – gaps in fences, help from fellow animals working in the fields nearby and through other farms. He issued orders to stop and expel anyone found crossing into the Farm except at the gate.

There were disturbing reports about young animals, babies even, sick, poor, escaping from the harshest of conditions at the worst farms run by humans. They were often sick when they arrived, after dangerous journeys, exploited by criminals, who abandoned them before they reached the gate. And they were locked up in tiny cages in the detention centre, in conditions even worse than those they were escaping.

The Barn of Dogs passed resolution after resolution and Lucia spoke regularly. 'Since the Revolution, Manor Farm has been renowned for its compassion. That's why we expelled the humans. We are better than this.' She employed lawyers who prepared cases for the Owls' Court challenging Mickey's instructions. Some of the decisions went against him. He retaliated by appointing as judges birds more sympathetic to his policies and by issuing redrafted laws that avoided the deficiencies identified by the owls.

Arguments about immigration distracted attention from the chaos of Mickey's presidency. He still did not have a full staff team. The normal business of government was barely functioning. One Chief of Staff had left and his replacement was rumoured to be on the verge of quitting.

Changes to the Farm also went largely unnoticed. During his presidency, Nelson had introduced organic farming and banned the use of pesticides. The results had been dramatic; improved crop and soil quality, reduced water use and increased demand for Manor Farm produce. Mickey was very much opposed to organic farming. He said it placed too many restrictions on the landowners and reduced production. That was true in the short term, but his predecessor had demonstrated the long term benefits. Nevertheless, he abolished bodies responsible for monitoring and regulating farming methods and health. Fields were not given fallow periods to rest and regenerate. And pesticides were reintroduced. All the gains of the Nelson era were lost. Workers' health was affected by the pesticides. Diego came home at the end of each day with his eyes burning and running. He accepted it stoically, because he knew it was a small sacrifice to get his family with him and to ensure they had a better life. Clara worried about his wellbeing. And, with an atmosphere of hostility to Pintos, she feared his wife and children might not be allowed in.

Eight

The swamp was at the western edge of the Farm, a place where no creature went except the frogs who lived there. Mickey's campaign promise to drain the swamp had been hard for the dogs to oppose. It was of little use to anyone except the frogs. As there were not many frogs, they had few votes. The proposal had clear benefits; if it could be drained and cleaned up, the land would be ideal grazing land, making the Farm wealthier. And everyone would be happy if there were fewer mosquitoes.

The dogs did not believe it would happen. Mickey had expected the presidency to be easy and he was disappointed at how hard it was to achieve implement his plans. As a business pig, he was used to squealing, grunting and oinking to get his own way. By contrast, government required tact, diplomacy and subtlety, qualities which Mickey neither possessed nor valued. He complained when he gave an order and it did not just happen. He failed to understand the separation of powers, the need to convince those tasked with implementing decisions and those who would be affected, to build a consensus, to demonstrate that changes would have a fair and equal effect, that the proposals would be effective and efficient, that money would not be wasted.

'I'm the President' he told his advisers. 'I can do what I like. Just do it.' That was why he could not retain staff. Either they tried to enact his wishes and failed or they knew what was needed and eventually gave up or angered him so much that he fired them. Lucia would have enjoyed his growing frustration and discomfort had she not known the terrible impact of his incompetence on the lives of ordinary animals.

And, despite the constant tweeting and bleating about swarms of immigrants flooding in, the Wall was delayed. Detailed, sensitive negotiations with the owners of land at the border took time. Mickey wanted the Pinto Farm owners to pay for the Wall, because it would help them to keep their animals in, but they refused in language as undiplomatic as his own. Then he spent weeks poring over colour charts, finally settling on black, announcing that the Wall would be the most beautiful wall ever. Companies owned by vocal Mickey supporters were given contracts to build parts of the ven if they had no experience in construction. Progress was slow.

To maintain momentum and support for the project, an event was organised at a place where the wall had been built to its full planned height. Mickey arrived to inspect it, surrounded by Rat News reporters. Crowds gathered to watch him and to see the new wall.

Bella could not hide her disappointment. 'It's just an ordinary wall. A big block of concrete painted black.'

'Yes it is' Clara replied. 'I don't want to stop animals coming here, especially not the ones who have suffered and are desperate for a better life. But, if I did, I'd want to do it properly. This wall is ridiculous. It won't work and there are much better things to spend money on.'

'I'm sure Mickey knows what he's doing' Bella said more to herself than to Clara.

Diego agreed that too many immigrants were coming to the Farm. He trusted Mickey to make sure the numbers were just right. Hardworking and loyal animals like him to be welcomed, but if too many of the wrong kind of animal came, there would not be enough for everyone to eat. Most animals wanted to come because it was so hard for them on their own Farms. He wished their lives could be improved, so they could be happier and more prosperous in their home environments. That would be for the best. Meanwhile, Diego hoped his family would reach the Farm before the Wall was completed, although he was confident his loyalty and hard work meant they would be allowed in anyway.

Nine

As each day passed, Lucia grew more worried. Mickey had fought the election on a platform of fighting corruption, but, once he took control, every big decision he made seemed to benefit either himself, his family or his associates.

She found out that a company had been given the contract to drain the swamp, apparently without skills or experience in the technical and difficult processes required. How could that have been allowed to happen? One of the few agencies to survive Mickey's cull controlled the approval of contracts and checking work was done properly. Despite the damage caused by ending organic farming, the experts still tried to maintain the delicate ecological balance needed for health and good crop growth. Mickey dismissed the head of the agency and replaced him with a friend who knew nothing about environmental matters. And this pig declared himself completely satisfied with the arrangements for draining the swamp. The frogs were driven off, but progress stalled. In any other time, this would have been a scandal, but it was hard to keep up with everything Mickey was doing.

He appealed to the basest instincts – fear and greed – and it was difficult to argue rationally against these emotions. So far, the majority were still prepared to go along with him, because the Farm was doing well. Although Lucia was certain this was Nelson's legacy and that the economy was going backwards under Mickey, many animals still believed he was making them wealthier. And the noise and aggression of his followers made it hard for dissenting voices to be heard.

It was not all going his way. Lucia took some comfort from a gradual but steady decline in his popularity. The frogs turned against him, fearing for their futures after their eviction from the swamp. Owners who had to give up their land for the Wall were angry, as were those who facing a shortage of farm labour as animals joined Wall construction teams. With tighter immigration controls, they would have to rely on local animals, who were held to be less hardworking than new arrivals. And persistent stories about Mickey's attitude towards female animals disturbed some of those who had voted for him. He said it was all lies spread by his enemies, but was it?

The chickens were gloomy. They were forced to work harder with less exercise and only permitted to keep a small number of eggs for hatching. Most eggs were exported, sold to humans to eat for their breakfast. And, although Mickey told Rat News their new cages were bigger and better, in fact they were smaller and uncomfortable.

The sheep still believed in him, but their confidence was increasingly fragile. They were thin. They were hungry. They were despondent. A few began to ask themselves whether all the promises were true. It was not enough for the majority to turn against Mickey, but their mood was starting to shift.

Ten

One night something so terrible happened, the animals feared the Farm would never be the same again.

The day had been quiet. No meetings. Just a hard day's work. An ordinary day.

When darkness fell, the animals bedded down for the night.

Nothing stirred. Not in the barns. Not in the stables, the coops, the pens, the burrows, the nests, the dens or the sheds. The only sounds were the trees blowing in the wind and the snoring, snorting and breathing of sleeping creatures.

No one heard the soft patter of paws, approaching carefully and stealthily, making their way from the woods, through the Farm until they reached the chicken coop.

Standing outside the coop, watching, waiting, ready to pounce, was a fox.   A young fox. Not a cub. A fully grown fox who had just reached adulthood. A fox who had attended Mickey's rallies. He had watched and listened, caught up in the excitement, impressed with a leader who understood him and his anger at the unfairness of his life. Like Mickey, he hated immigrants. But most of all he blamed the dogs, animals who ought to be his brothers. From their luxurious kennels, they looked down on foxes who lived in the woods. Foxes were rarely given the opportunity to work on the farm, instead having to scavenge for scraps. No wonder some turned to crime.

This particular fox was unpopular with his fellow foxes. He tried his best to make friends, but he was a little odd, so they would never spend time with him and barely even spoke to him. In desperation, he reached out to other species. Not dogs of course, because he knew they would have nothing to do with him. He tried horses, llamas, donkeys and goats, all without success. Once or twice, he chatted to a cow or a sheep, but it never led to anything. The smaller animals and birds were scared of him, a legacy of the time before the Revolution when foxes hid in the woods and came out to kill and eat cats, rabbits, rats, mice and birds. Those foxes who still wanted to do that had left the Farm and gone to other places. His family and others like them stopped killing their fellow creatures so they could stay.

One day he struck up a conversation with some chickens who he came across roaming in the fields. They seemed to like him and he trotted happily back home to the woods. The next day, eager to meet up with his new friends, he hurried straight to where he had seen them. They were there, but so was a large hen. As soon as she saw him, she called to the chickens, telling them foxes were dangerous and they should stay away from him.

He was heartbroken. He felt lonely and isolated with no hope for the future. Every day he got angrier. One night he could not sleep. He could not take any more. He hated everyone, but he particularly hated the chickens. How dare an inferior species reject him. He still loved Mickey, believing he was making things better for animals like him who had been left behind. He was convinced Mickey would approve of his decision to take direct action. 'I'll show them' he said to himself. 'I'll make those chickens pay for what they've done to me.'

So he crept from the woods in the middle of the night when everyone was asleep. He dug his way under the fence and entered the coop. He struck hard and fast, growling, snarling, biting, tearing. His victims pecked at him, trying desperately to save themselves. His anger exploded and he lost all control. The noise woke all the chickens, who clucked, squawked and crowed in fear and terror. Blood and feathers everywhere. Chickens lay dead and dying.

The cages made it harder to get away, but some managed to fly out. Other animals were woken by the commotion. Once they realised what was happening, they raced to the coop. Right at the front, galloping at full speed was Diego. Without a thought for his safety, he threw himself at the fox, who turned, wild and savage, raging uncontrollably, sinking his teeth into the llama's neck. Diego reacted instinctively, kicking, spitting, neck wrestling, chest ramming and biting. Clara and Bella waited with the other animals, watching, desperately hoping he would win. Because this was a fight to the death.

Chickens ran around, some flying, others trying to peck at the fox. But it was impossible. The two creatures clung to each other as they span round, like a single wild beast, blood spraying, howling with pain and anger. Eventually, the movement slowed and then stopped. They lay motionless on the ground. Clara and Bella ran up. The fox was dead, his eyes staring sightlessly. Diego was alive, barely, his fur ripped and bleeding, his eyes closed.

They carried him back to his stable, lay him on the hay and bathed his wounds. Clara and Bella sat by his side until morning, stroking his face.

Eleven

In the morning, there was an eery silence across the Farm. The animals were deeply shocked, too shocked to speak. In total, fifteen chickens had been murdered in the massacre.

Everyone knew the death toll would have been far worse without Diego's bravery. He was a great hero. And he was still alive. Exhausted and injured, but he lived. A vet was called and he tended to his wounds and gave him antibiotics to prevent infection. He was expected to make a full recovery, but he would need to rest to regain his strength.

The arrival of Mickey's officials to count the dead, remove the bodies and arrange for the chicken coop to be cleaned reminded everyone that no pigs had been seen during the massacre or afterwards. There were mutterings of discontent, even from the sheep.

The pigeons reported back and Mickey's spokespig was despatched to explain. She said 'Our homes are the farthest away from the chicken coop. Unfortunately, all the pigs slept through the whole sad episode. Of course, had Mickey known what was happening, he would have been at the front, bravely risking his life to save his animals.'

Shock and sorrow were the main emotions across the Farm, but there was anger at the murderer, at foxes in general and at the pigs for not protecting the chickens. A meeting was hastily organised. Mickey attended and spoke.

Clara expected him to confer an honour on Diego for his heroism. Although he mentioned him briefly, he spent most of his speech declaring that foxes were 'fine animals' and the culprit was 'very sick and deserving of pity'. She was furious. Mickey was always quick to criticise animals who had immigrated from Pinto Farm when they committed even the most minor misdemeanours. Now it seemed his hatred was so great he could not even recognise a Pinto immigrant llama who had saved lives in his adopted farm.

Perhaps even worse was his attitude to the chicken community. He mentioned the dead chickens, offering his thoughts and prayers. But he majored on the impact on the Farm's economy of the drop in egg production, rather than the terror and grief at the loss of their loved ones. He advised the chickens to stay in the coop so as not to put themselves at risk and refused appeals for guards to be on duty outside the coop every night. As the White Barn was surrounded by guards at all times and there were regular patrols across all pig residences, Clara understood that, to Mickey and his followers, only pigs' lives mattered.

Twelve

Mickey's followers were out in force, repeating his words to counter criticisms of their idol. This was just one isolated troubled fox, most crime was committed by immigrants and the greatest loss was of future egg laying capacity.

Unsurprisingly, the chickens were not happy. It was not only the massacre and the disregard for their security. Cramped cages and restrictions on their movement and leisure time combined to convince them they were less valued than other animals.

Nelson made a rare speech, arguing persuasively for chickens to be protected. His compassion for animalkind shone through. He asked the question that was on the lips of many animals. 'Why is Mickey not prepared to spend the Farm's money on keeping chickens safe?'

As complaints about his presidency increased, Mickey's behaviour became more extreme. He still wound up the crowd to chant 'Lock her up' even though Jess was rarely seen or heard. He also directed his anger against Lucia, the puppies and any animal that challenged him. Worryingly for him, although those who came were increasingly passionate, attendance at the meetings was dropping. The pigs had to be seen there to avoid his wrath. Most of the sheep still went. Of course, the pigeons were always there, ready to fly around the Farm afterwards tweeting his latest messages. But attendance by other species was dropping. When he recovered, even Diego wondered whether he should go. In the end he did, but he felt disappointed that few animals remembered his part in rescuing the chickens.

Mickey was not a happy pig. He kept losing his temper. 'I'm the greatest leader the Farm has ever had' he shouted. 'It's only because of all the fake news that my tremendous achievements are not recognised.'

He blamed 'nasty' animals like Loopy Lucia and Slack Jack. It was rumoured that he spent hours in his den at the White Barn, preparing tweets for his pigeon friends and listening to Rat News, his favourite radio station. He refused to speak to CNN and other stations and repeatedly attacked them and their reporting.

His behaviour was erratic and even some of the pigs closest to him were getting worried. Questions were asked, never in his presence. Was there something wrong with him? Could he be ill either physically or mentally? Stories leaked from the White Barn about how his staff were struggling. Anyone who challenged him was fired. The only way his senior officials could keep the Farm running at all was by not telling him what they were doing.

Thirteen

As Mickey's behaviour worsened, the contrast with his predecessor could not have been starker both in style and substance. Whereas Nelson had been cautious and conscientious, Mickey ruled by impulse and whim. His decisions – tax cuts, appointments to posts, working arrangements – always benefitted himself, his family or his coterie. But with no major scandals and the unwavering support of the Barn of Pigs, he seemed unassailable.

That changed when rumours started to spread about interference by Soy Farm in the election. If this were true, it could cause Mickey serious damage. The catalyst was one of his advisers, who let slip in a drunken moment that Mickey's campaign team had been talking to the Soys both before and after the election.

There had to be an investigation. Initially, Mickey said he did not object, because he had nothing to hide. But then he fired the head of the Farm Beast Investigation Service (FBIS), an organisation set up to protect and defend Manor Farm by upholding and enforcing its criminal laws. The FBIS not only had to do what its mission required, but it had to be seen to do it fairly and without favour, regardless of who was leading the Farm at the time. The investigation was led by a well-respected elder of the community, a pig called Willie, who set to work straight away, studying papers, putting a team together and interviewing witnesses and suspects. The inquiry was long and laborious. Willie made no public statements, so no one knew what he was learning.

News stories were speculation based on farmyard gossip; the animals talked of little else. The three friends tried not to fall out even though they did not agree with each other. Clara was sure Willie would find enough to destroy Mickey. Bella accepted that the Soys had tried to influence the election, but she could not believe Mickey was involved. Diego had faith in justice and fairness on the Farm, so whatever the outcome, it would be the right one.

It looked bad for Mickey when members of his team, animals central to his election campaign, were arrested and charged with criminal offences. The owls had spent the Nelson years hunting for insects and fish and sleeping. Now they were busy judging all day. The small prison barn was so full, there was talk of opening another one.

Apparently, the Soys had trained animals who were sent to Manor Farm to influence the outcome of the election. They mingled with their own breeds, spread fake stories, infiltrated Jess's campaign so her plans and messages could be quickly countered and even voted although they were not Manor citizens. Since the Revolution, independent elections had been a key element of ensuring that humans could never return. The charges faced by Mickey's campaign staff were horrifying. They were accused of conspiring with another Farm, which was a serious offence. And, as Mickey had beaten Jess by a small margin, it would be a great scandal if his victory was only achieved by Soy interference.

Mickey was a friend of Soy Farm's leader, Ivan. Unlike Mung, he defended Soy whenever it was criticised. The big questions were 'Did he know what the Soys were doing? And did he know his staff were involved?

Fourteen

Mickey's initial reaction was to denounce the Soy conspiracy as a hoax started by the dogs because they refused to accept the election result.

'Hoax' tweeted the pigeons. 'Fake news by Loopy Lucia and Slack Jack'.

This convinced the sheep, but few other animals. Even some pigs had doubts, but they were too scared of Mickey and his fawning followers to speak out. Gradually his position changed. He still maintained that he had won the election fair and square, but he claimed he barely knew or could not remember those members of his team who were charged with crimes. That was odd, because Clara and the other donkeys, who everyone knew had the best memories in the Farm, remembered seeing them at campaign meetings, standing right next to him. Even those creatures with poor memories recognised their faces as they were led to the Barn jail.

Most troubling of all was that Mickey seemed not to accept the rule of law. He threatened to use his presidential powers to pardon any animal who had been convicted. And he complained constantly about the owls, saying they were biased against him. He particularly hated one old owl, who was highly respected, close to retirement and known to be in ill health. He tried to force her to retire. The dogs admired her strength as she vowed to keep going to prevent him appointing an owl ally in her place.   His owl supporters, few in number and the least intelligent of their species, would do as he told them. Where would that leave the checks and balances that were the foundation of successful government and democracy on the Farm?

Finally Willie's report was received.   He concluded that the Soys had interfered in the Farm's Presidential vote. That had been welcomed by Mickey's campaign team, some of whom had business links with Ivan's associates or had accepted donations from friends of Ivan. Amongst those charged with crimes and sent to the prison barn were some very important pigs. Although there was insufficient evidence of a criminal conspiracy with the Soys, Willie concluded that Mickey had obstructed justice by trying to influence the investigation. Mickey's appointee as Head of the FBIS, who was Willie's boss, ruled that a sitting President could not be charged with a criminal offence. This was all very confusing. Was he innocent or was he guilty?

Bella's opinion, which she did her best to explain to a sceptical Clara, was probably representative of the majority. 'Mickey's the President and leader of the Farm. I support him' she said, although Clara had noticed that she rarely wore her MMGA hat these days. 'I really hope he did nothing wrong and he didn't know what was going on. Even if he did, I'm sure he did everything for good reasons. He's still the right pig for the job.' She was sure he would be more careful in future.

But that was not what happened. Instead Mickey proclaimed that he was fully vindicated and he fired everyone he believed to be less than 100% loyal. He held more rallies, three times a week, shouting to the faithful about smears, lies and the treachery of the dogs. For those who had always doubted his suitability for high office, the idea that Mickey was emboldened rather than chastened by the investigation was terrifying.

Fifteen

If Mickey had hoped that criticisms of his leadership would stop with the end of the investigation, he was soon disappointed. Lucia and the dogs kept up their accusations of incompetence and corruption and rumours of wrongdoing and unpredictable behaviour swept the Farm.

As all farm animals knew, mud sticks. He fought back in two ways.

Firstly, he attacked his opponents. He used nicknames to ridicule them – Loony Lucia and Cracked Jack. And he castigated others for the very same offences of which he had been accused – corruption, conspiring with the Soys, hiding money and failing to pay taxes.

Secondly, he puffed himself up and granted himself honours that Nelson had given to animals who had done remarkable things. Mickey held ceremonies attended by his supporters, at which he was awarded Stable Genius, Kennel of Truth, Mighty Pen and Shed of State. The most extreme Sugar Candy Mountain believers said he had been sent to them from the summit. Clara was disgusted. 'How can anyone take them seriously? They believe in unicorns' she sneered. That was slightly unfair. Mickey's greatest raven supporters enriched themselves by fooling the poorest and most gullible animals. But others genuinely tried to help those most in need and preached that the way to reach the Sugar Candy Mountain was to be and to do good. These birds would never support him.

The chickens' anger was intensifying. Their leader, Frederick, spoke of their loyalty and hard work. Instead of relaxing outside in the fields, they spent almost all day in cages with little air, water or food. 'We never complained. We did it for the good of the Farm.' The cocks hardly slept, because their job was to get everyone on the Farm up for their shifts. They could be heard crowing through the day and night. And, of course, the chickens had suffered the terrible massacre. That had been the turning point in their attitude to Mickey. They knew pigs thought they were superior to them, but they were not his enemies.

Frederick reminded the animals of the massacre. 'So many of our fellow chickens died. It was an unprovoked attack by a vicious fox. And we were saved by our magnificent friend, Diego the llama. But what's happened since then? Our rations have been cut, our egg targets increased, forced to spend our lives in cages. That's not what we voted for. Mickey – please help us. Don't forget us chickens and our sacrifices. We want to be part of your project, not its victims.'

It was a great speech and the chickens clucked in agreement. Lucia was quick to congratulate him and not just because she agreed with every word. She had her eye on the next election. Few chickens had voted for Mickey last time, but a high turnout for Jack would give him a real chance of victory. By contrast, Mickey paid tribute to the heroic chickens and their hard work for the good of all. But he feared they were being let down by their treacherous leaders. He named no names, but he did not need to. He announced an increase in rations and an additional 10 minutes a day to exercise out in the fields for his great chicken friends. But the chickens did not feel any fuller or fitter. Had the rations really been increased? Was the exercise period really longer? That is what Mickey had promised. No one had the courage to check.

Sixteen

The events that followed were difficult for all but the cleverest animals to understand.

Two nearby farms, Soy and Chickpea, were in constant conflict with each other. Chickpea accused Soy of sending its humans and animals into Chickpea territory. Soy retaliated by claiming that their natives living in Chickpea were badly treated. Clara's reading of history was that there was right and wrong on both sides and this kind of fighting and arguing benefitted no one. It was the ordinary humans and animals on both farms who suffered, never their leaders.

Mickey's policy was to trade with both Farms. No one really opposed that. Many animals from Manor Farm had links with Soy and Chickpea and did business with them. The problems started when it emerged that Jack's son, Chase, was based in Chickpea and he had made a lot of money.

Who could have guessed that so much trouble could start with a little mouse? Unlike rats, mice were not respected for their intelligence. Most of the time they were simply ignored. What no one realised was that they hid under floors, behind trees and in holes, listening, observing, taking it all in. Before the revolution, humans assumed all animals were stupid, so they failed to notice Major inspiring them to rebellion. In exactly the same way, the pigs, dogs, everyone really, underestimated the mice, who were canny little creatures.

One mouse was fed up to his molars with Mickey's promises and the punishment meted out when the mice supplemented their meagre rations by gnawing on crops in the fields. One day, he went to the FBIS and reported hearing a conversation between Lorenzo, Mickey's personal lawyer, and the owner of Chickpea farm. He said Lorenzo demanded a full investigation into Chase's activities in Chickpea. If this was refused, he threatened to end all trade between the two farms. As Chickpea was dependent on Manor Farm for nuts and seeds, this put them in a difficult position.

Fearful of the consequences, the mouse asked to remain anonymous, but the substance of his story was widely reported. Once the word was out, another mouse came forward and said he had heard similar conversations. Could Mickey be so nervous about the popularity of Jack, his rival at the next election, that he would attack him through his son? Were he and his henchpigs prepared to threaten leaders of other would be a gross breach of the constitution, a serious crime.

The young pups and their supporters were desperate to bring Mickey before the Barn of Dogs and charge him with treason. Lucia was cautious as ever. 'I'm sure it's true, but where's the evidence? If we could be sure of convicting him, I'd be the first to say we should go for it. But it's only hearsay, from a couple of mice who are too scared to make their allegations in public.'

'But we can force him out.'

'I doubt it.' She had been around for many years and understood that the President controlled the levers of power and communication. Patiently, she explained again. 'If we fail, we'll be blamed for causing trouble and not respecting the result of the election. And that will make it much harder to beat him next time.'

In the end, her paw was forced, not by the clamour from the puppies, but by Mickey's shameless reaction. He said there was nothing wrong with getting damaging information on his opponents from other Farms and nothing wrong with using it. Eventually she could take no more and she announced that charges would be brought against him.

Seventeen

'Loony Lucia,' tweeted the pigeons. 'It's a conspiracy' bleated those sheep who were strong enough to be out bleating. 'Any animals supporting this travesty will be denied entry to the Sugar Candy Mountain' announced Mickey's chief raven supporter. But once she had decided, Lucia was a tough and resolute bitch.

The Barn of Dogs organised meetings and called witnesses. Mickey did not recognise their authority, so he refused to attend to put his case. His lappig, Lorenzo, put his arguments for him, not in the Barn, but on Rat News. 'This is nothing but desperate lies by sad dogs who can't bear to lose power.' He made vague allegations about Nelson being responsible for corruption and conspiracies with other farms, but the details were never clear enough to be investigated. Clara, watching from the sidelines, and Lucia, in the barns of government, saw it as a smear, a distraction to draw attention away from the charges. And then new rumours reached the animals that Lorenzo himself had business dealings in Chickpea. If that were true, no wonder he tried to shift blame to Nelson.

After hearing all the evidence, the Barn of Dogs voted to remove Mickey as President. The law required the case to be taken to the Barn of Pigs. Only if he was found guilty by both Barns would he be removed from the presidency.

Bella found the whole affair distressing. She did not know who or what to believe. 'I'll wait and see what happens when it gets to the Barn of Pigs'. Clara was certain of his guilt, but she did not believe the Pigs would convict one of their own. She said nothing. Sometimes that was the wisest thing to do.

The Barn of Pigs was packed with Mickey's supporters. He was not called to give evidence and they decided not to hear any witnesses.

Bella was shocked. 'How can they try a case without hearing any witnesses?' she asked.

Clara was not surprised. Mickey was so confident about his position, so sure he was always right, that he believed he was answerable to no one. She was pinning her hopes on him getting what he deserved at the next election, a trouncing by the dogs' candidate Jack. Until then, she hoped Lucia would limit the damage caused by his presidency.

Clara was right. The Pigs showed no interest in the evidence presented to them, snorting impatiently and whispering among themselves until they could take the vote and end it all. Only one pig, Rod, took a different line. 'This is truly horrifying' he said after he had heard the case for the prosecution 'I was elected to do the best for the Farm. That's more important than who the President happens to be at any time.' When the vote was taken, he was the only pig to vote for Mickey's removal. All the rest voted against. No action was to be taken against Mickey. The case was not proven. And for ever after, Rod was ignored by all the pigs.

Eighteen

Mickey had won an election using cheap slogans. His strategy for the next one was to keep to simple messages: the need to protect Manor Farm from the twin threats of immigrants from Pinto and the unfair trading practices of Mung, both of which could only be defeated if he beat his enemies. The reality was that the Farm's reputation had been at its height when Nelson was in charge. He argued the opposite, saying that Nelson was corrupt and weak and that respect depended on showing strength. It seemed truth no longer mattered.

The Wall was still his greatest priority. At every rally, he shook his fist and shouted 'Build the wall' and his supporters chanted it back at him. The pigeons flew all over the Farm afterwards tweeting 'Build the wall.' Many animals believed that a Wall built by a strong leader would protect them from harm, from invaders who threatened their way of life and well-being.

Clara grunted. 'The animals making the most fuss about the Wall are the ones with nothing to lose.' But when she thought hard about it, she realised that they did have something to lose – their self-respect. Mickey was not clever, but he tapped into the psyches of the weak and the dispossessed. He said what they wanted to hear or, at least, what they thought they wanted to hear once he had said it.

Reports on Rat News reassured them that good progress was being made on building the Wall. So what if his friends and family were being given the contracts; what mattered was that it would protect them all. The sheep were convinced, the pigs squealed their support and even cows, horses and goats were impressed.

Loud noises could be heard as the builders blasted out the earth and started to lay the foundations. The animals visited most evenings to see how the work was going. Soon sections of the Wall emerged, tall and imposing, at strategic points along the border to Pinto Farm. Here was a leader who did what he promised, who looked after them. That many of the bad animals, like the fox responsible for the chicken massacre, were home grown, was almost forgotten.

One evening after dinner, a large group strolled along to the border to see how it looked. As the animals at the front came within sight of the site, there were audible gasps and cries. Clara, Bella and Diego, nearer the back, were confused.

'What's that all about? Is something wrong?'

The cries were growing louder as they pushed their way to the front. 'No way. This can't be true.'

Clara gasped when she realised where they were and what they were looking at. The orchard was the site of a barn where Major had spoken of his dream of taking the Farm from the humans. His body was buried in the orchard, a stone carved with his name marked the spot and commemorated the father of the revolution, the founder of the Farm. Every year on the anniversary of the revolution, all the animals came together at a ceremony to remember him. She looked around her. The orchard was changed, disturbed, the trees gone. Where was Major's headstone? Where was his name? It was all gone. All that was left was a large open hole.

The dogs were furious and almost all the animals, even some of the braver pigs. Mickey was initially unrepentant, but rising fury meant he had to call a barn meeting. He argued that the safety and security of the Farm was more important than a memorial to a long dead animal. His followers were impressed, but most animals could not overlook the desecration of a holy place. Surely, they asked themselves and each other, the Wall could have been diverted a little to avoid Major's grave. Even if meant going into Pinto Farm, the Pintos would never have dared to challenge the mighty Manor Farm.

Nelson was appalled at the lack of respect shown to the Farm's history and one of its greatest heroes. He organised his own meeting at which he paid homage to Major and his legacy.

Unusually, Mickey changed his position in the face of mounting criticism. He said it was all the fault of the Director of Construction, a pig he barely knew, which was odd because he had appointed him. 'Mickey never met him' tweeted the pigeons. He fired the pig, who defended himself, saying he had only done what he was told. He even had plans approved by Mickey. But his voice was drowned out. He went back to his pen and was not heard of again.

Some animals vowed never to support Mickey again, but most accepted that the Construction Director had disobeyed orders.

A plaque with Major's name on it was hastily put up on the wall of the barn he had lived in, but it was rarely visited and the annual commemoration ceremony did not happen again.

Nineteen

Mickey loved the pomp and circumstance of power. He had no sense of history, preferring to concentrate on the present (his great leadership) rather than the past (his predecessors).

He instituted a series of dinners to which he invited leaders of other Farms and the heads of companies with whom (coincidentally) he, his friends and family did business. Humans from outside were brought in to prepare and serve the food with help from Manor Farm animals. The arrivals and departures in grand carriages and cars were a highlight for those who would never be important enough to receive invitations.

The biggest and most important dinner was held on the anniversary of Mickey's election victory, an auspicious occasion. Soy Farm's leader, Ivan, was invited which showed just how important the date was.

Bella was asked to assist. 'It's such an honour' she gushed, even though Clara warned her it would be exhausting after a day's work.

She was tired when she reached the White Barn, but excitement and anticipation reinvigorated her. All the guests looked smart and beautiful.

'What a wonderful time to live' she thought. 'And how lucky we are to share in the prosperity of the Farm.' When she had said this to Clara, her friend had asked her what her share was. She did not have the answer, but it had to be true, because Mickey said it was so and he was Making Manor Farm Great Again. Although she had reservations about some of his behaviour, she still wanted to believe that.

She was not allowed in the kitchen. With her big body and hooves, that made absolute sense. The humans loaded the food into shiny silver dishes and brought them out on trolleys. She pushed a heavy trolley into the magnificent dining hall and stepped back as the human waiters lifted the lids and started to serve.

She looked at the floor, too respectful to stare at the guests while they ate. Then her nostrils started to twitch. What was that smell? It smelled good. It smelled sweet. But what was it? She started to feel uneasy. She could not stop herself looking. And what she saw made her jump. The head waiter turned and glared at her. She kept completely still until the work began again. The overpowering aromas of alcohol and sweet desserts were intoxicating, but the memory of what she had smelled before was vivid and painful.

Bella was an honest cow. For the first time in her life, she stole something. As the dinner ended and the pigs and humans left to return to their homes, she sneaked into the kitchen and took a menu. No reason not to. It would only be thrown away. Still she felt bad as she hid it in her coat and went back to her shed.

She lay awake all night, too stressed to sleep. The following morning she took the menu to Clara and asked her to read it. Clara was silent, unable to speak for a few seconds. When she spoke, Bella understood Clara's shock and her own fears were confirmed. The main course, the one she was worried about, the one that smelled so good, was lamb. Lamb. Confused and distressed, she tried to work it out. Several sheep had left the Farm in recent weeks and Mickey said they had gone to other farms to work there and to sell their wool. Now she realised it was all lies. They had been sent to one of the meat processing plants that all animals feared. If it was not bad enough that Mickey and his cronies profited from the death of their fellow creatures, they had eaten them.

Twenty

Diego was excited. He had heard from his wife.
She and their children were on their way from
Pinto Farm.

Already working hard, now he worked even
harder. He kept his stall as tidy as he could,
getting help from Bella to decorate it. His wife
was an independent creature, a clever scientist,
not a little female who stayed at home while her
stud was out working, but she loved to live in a
clean and comfortable stall. They had missed
each other desperately. He could not wait to be
with her again and to see his son and daughter.
They had been so small when he left. Would
they remember him? What did they look like
now?

Diego did not have a calendar or a watch. Nor
would it have helped if he had, because he could
not read or tell the time. He could hardly bear
the wait. He was pleased to have the
opportunity to work long hours, so he would
have a good stock of provisions when they
arrived. During the day, he visualised his new
life with his beautiful family with him every day.
The nights were even more joyful. In his
dreams, the stall was bigger and brighter, the
rations more generous, the Farm more

prosperous and their futures rosier. He could hardly contain himself.

How long would it take them to reach the Farm? Every morning he woke feeling hopeful and went to sleep slightly disappointed but happy that, with each day, their arrival was getting closer. As time passed, he started to feel uneasy. Was he worrying unnecessarily? He knew Mickey's troops were tough on immigrants, but he was a good and loyal citizen and the hero of the chicken massacre. He had passed on his family's details and had been assured that they would be fine. Nothing could go wrong, could it?

Another day. Another night. Another day.

He was out in the fields when Bella rushed up and told him to come quickly. She did not say why, but she looked upset. Panicking, he galloped home to his stable. What he found was a mystifying sight. A female who looked like his wife, but with none of her verve or energy. Her fur was wet and dirty, her eyes dripping with tears, terrified, pleading.

When she spoke, he knew for certain that she was his wife, but her voice was soft, barely audible as she repeated over and over again 'I'm so sorry. I'm so sorry…'

Twenty One

Diego trotted up to his wife, moving closer until they were touching. He could feel her body trembling. 'What's happened?' he asked. 'Please tell me.'

She hesitated, inhaling and exhaling slowly, trying to calm herself before she was able to continue. The story she told him was so horrific, he could scarcely believe what he was hearing.

Between sobs, she said 'We crossed Pinto Farm and then walked north until we reached the border gate. The guards stopped us. I told them we were coming to join our husband and father, Diego. That you were a Farm resident and loyal citizen, a hero who saved the chickens. They laughed in my face and said no Pinto llama would ever be a hero on their Farm.'

She had heard stories of the camps immigrants were held in until they were either sent back to Pinto or allowed in. 'I expected we'd be held somewhere warm and dry with enough food and water.' She stopped and calmed herself before she could go on. Diego realised he was holding his breath.

'It was terrible. Worse than I could ever have imagined. They took the children away. My camp was for adults only. We did not get enough to eat. Nowhere to wash. And we were squashed into tiny sheds. Some animals had been there for months waiting for their cases to be considered.'

They were all miserable and distressed, but determined to make it to Manor Farm where they believed hard work would be rewarded with comfort and companionship.   If only they were allowed in. And all parents were desperate to see their children again. Weak, exhausted from long hard journeys and with overcrowded and filthy living conditions, disease soon spread. The guards reacted with disgust, pushing them away, beating them back when they begged for help.

Bella was listening, her large eyes glistening with tears. Diego was too stunned to react.

'I caught the disease' she continued. 'I got really sick. When I was recovering, a guard came for me one night. He said he was there when you rescued the chickens. He wanted to help me. He took me to another camp so I could be with the children.'

But she was alone now. Where were his children?

She stopped and looked at him. He glanced away, the pain in her eyes too much for him to bear. She went on. 'When I found them, they were both very ill. I pleaded with the guards to call a vet. Eventually the good guard brought one who gave them medication. I was still very weak, but I nursed the children day and night. I had to.'

Gradually their daughter's condition improved, but their son got sicker and sicker. Two nights ago, she sat up all night watching him, his little chest rising and falling as he struggled to breathe. His breathing grew slower and shallower until it stopped. He was dead. 'Our son is dead. Diego I'm so sorry.'

When morning came, the guards told her that their application for entry had been approved. It was too late for their little cria. All she could do was to bring her daughter as soon as she was well enough to travel. Still not fully fit, she was being treated by a vet, but expected to recover.

Diego was numb. How could his beloved son be dead? He had come to the Farm to make a better life for his family. He knew he was neither a pig nor a Manor native, but he was a higher beast. And he had worked as hard as he could. He had treated everyone with respect. He had made friends. He had rescued the chickens. How could this happen?

He pressed his body closer to his wife, not to reassure her, but to share her pain.

Twenty Two

As more animals criticised his leadership, Mickey hit back. Blaming fake news started by evil dogs, he repeated how wonderfully he was running the Farm. He said he had done more than any President ever in the entire history of the Farm for the pigs, the sheep, even the dogs, the goats, the horses, the cows, the chickens, all the creatures on the Farm. He did not feel the love he deserved.

Many creatures did not see it the same way. The chickens in particular were getting angrier. Their hard work and egg laying was not appreciated and they were treated as second class citizens. Chickens never lived long enough to have the same sense of history as donkeys, so their leader, Frederick, went to Clara and asked what she knew. She told him what she thought; that their lives were no better than when the Farm was run by humans before the Revolution.

Frederick asked for a meeting with Mickey. He intended to explain his concerns and to propose improvements. Making the chickens happier and more productive would benefit the whole farm. He was disappointed at how hard it was to get an appointment to see Mickey and then two meetings were cancelled at the last minute. A peaceful and moderate cock, the contempt shown to his species made him so furious that he spoke publicly of injustice and the need for love and respect for all animals.

Mickey hit back, calling Frederick and the chickens traitors whose disloyalty was preventing the Farm from becoming Great Again. This was the last straw. They came out on strike, refusing to produce eggs. In return, he cut their rations, just as Napoleon had done after the Revolution. They were determined to hold out, but that was impossible when they were starving. Frederick requested a meeting again, this time to broker a settlement, but Mickey refused. 'This' he said 'is about law and order. The chickens have to stop protesting and go back to work.'

The rebellion ended when nine chickens starved to death, the same number that had died when their ancestors revolted against Napoleon. They had no choice; they went back to work, so weak and miserable that it took weeks for egg production to return to normal. Production was already down compared to the high levels experienced under Nelson. In a series of increasingly aggressive speeches, Mickey attacked the chickens. Then he sold Frederick and the most militant chickens to other farms and they were never heard of again.

Twenty Three

The plight of the chickens was soon forgotten as news reached the Farm about a disease. Rat News reported that it was a new illness known as the Halo Virus, which originated on Mung Farm. It was not confined to any single species and the death rate was much higher than for more common illnesses like avian and swine flu. And it was not just Mung Farm. Cases had been reported everywhere and it was spreading fast.

A very clever elderly pig called Fussy had advised leaders of the Farm about medical matters for as long as anyone could remember. He was well respected by dogs, pigs and all the animals. He also worked closely with the Interfarm Health Organisation (IHO), through which he obtained information on the new illness. He was seen entering the White Barn on several occasions, but he remained tight lipped when asked what he was doing there.

The Barn of Dogs held a debate. They called scientists and those who had experience of problems on other farms. Lucia was particularly worried.

'This is a big threat, not only to this Farm but to animalkind' she said. 'We have to protect ourselves as best we can, starting with closing all Farm borders and movement around the Farm.' This was neither controversial nor brilliant: it was what other farms had done and what Fussy was said to be recommending. The dogs barked their agreement. But Mickey scoffed, ignoring all warnings. He called a meeting. Curious and fearful of the future, more animals than ever attended, crowding into the barn and spilling out on to the grass outside, expecting to hear from him what he planned to do to protect them from this frightening illness. Instead, he responded angrily.

'This is a witch hunt, a plot by the dogs to cause trouble. There is no terrible illness. Not here. There may be a little problem on Mung Farm, but we all know how badly their farm is run. No wonder they have disease. But here we have the best doctors, the best science, the best cleanliness. No one will catch it here. I can promise you that.'

Many animals were relieved. Even the chickens felt better now they did not have to add worry about illness to their problems. But Lucia and the other senior dogs were not reassured. Despite boasting about his natural ability as a scientist, Mickey had never studied anything. Why would they listen to him rather than the

IHO, Fussy and reports from neighbouring farms? Lucia tried to make preparations, to reopen Nelson's hospital, to build up supplies of medication and cleaning materials and to organise the Farm to keep animals safe and fed and to protect the weakest. Her priority was to save lives.

Mickey scoffed. He had it all under control, even though he never specified how. 'It's a plot. A hoax' he repeated. 'It's all about Loony Lucia and Cracked Jack trying to bring me down. Fake news. Desperate behaviour by desperate creatures.'

And so it was until one day when a cow was found lying in a field, coughing, in pain, with a high fever and too weak to move. The Halo Virus had reached the Farm.

Twenty Four

The cow, a sweet quiet and popular figure, was taken back to her shed where she lay, sick and scared for a week. When she started to recover, her bull was delighted. The cows were delighted. The whole farm was delighted. Mickey bragged that he had been proved right; the illness was nothing. Only one case, when other Farms had had many. He had protected them.

Then the bull succumbed. He got much sicker than his wife. A vet was called, but he was too sick to be treated at home. With no hospital on the Farm, he had to be collected and taken to a hospital outside. There was no word about his condition for a week and then his cow was informed that he had died.

Four more bulls and 2 cows also caught the illness. And mice and horses who either visited the cowsheds or lived nearby were reported to be showing symptoms.

The mood on the Farm changed. How could the disease be under control when it was spreading? And wasn't every animal at risk?

Fussy appeared at a meeting with Mickey. He had insisted that it was attended only by representatives of each species rather than an all animal meeting which he deemed too dangerous. He talked about shielding, about isolation, about distancing. 'Stay in your barns, sheds and pens' he advised. 'Don't go to work unless it's essential. Only go out if you have to, to get provisions. Don't get too close to any other animal.' Mickey nodded sagely.

Lucia was frightened. Before the Revolution, humans had the benefit of scientific knowledge, which she knew had developed considerably since then. Now Manor Farm had little of its own expertise, so it depended instead on the IHO. Not that animals were ignorant. Many pigs had studied and qualified as scientists. Some goats and horses too. But Mickey said he had no need for experts. 'I know as much as any of them, more even. All scientists are amazed by how much I know. I've got an instinct for it.' Lucia thought he had no instincts for anything except how to exploit situations for his own advantage and for self-publicity.

The virus was spreading. Soy Farm had many cases. Information was hard to come by because Ivan would not release the figures, but the number of deaths was said to be high.

Mung Farm finally got the illness under control. No one would rely on any figures they released, but the IHO was satisfied that the outbreak was coming to an end. There was still a threat of a second wave, but they were constantly learning about the disease, how it worked, who suffered most and why. Scientists were developing treatments and analysing their effectiveness and even working on a vaccine. There was a long was to go, but every day progress was made. Working together was the best way of beating the disease. The Head of the IHO said 'We are as strong as our weakest farm'.

But Mickey was not prepared to work with others. Manor First was his mantra as he redoubled his attacks on Mung Farm. The dogs agreed it was important to find out why the Halo Virus had started there. One rumour was that unrefrigerated meat which was then fed to other animals could be the cause. The dogs had long suspected animal products were slipped into the feed at Manor Farm, but they had no evidence. Mickey denied it, but they did not believe him.

He shifted his position and it was easy to see why. With the illness spreading, he could no longer argue that the pandemic was a hoax. He looked worried and with good reason. Other farms were locking down, but that had a swift and brutal impact on their economies. The election was imminent. Elections were won and lost on the economy. All animals knew that. Some said he was considering letting the disease spread unchecked until the Farm was protected by herd immunity. That did not impress the cows. But in the end, he understood that he had to show he cared about saving lives. Weighing up alternatives and considering advice was not his strength. Eventually and reluctantly, he agreed to a lockdown, but he made it clear that Manor would open again as soon as it was safe. He would be the judge of when that was.

Twenty Five

Despite the lockdown, the number of cases on the Farm continued to rise. Reports from other farms were of multiple deaths, mainly but not exclusively older animals.

The sickest were taken away to hospitals outside. 'Why did Mickey close Nelson's hospital?' was the question whispered in barns, pens and sheds. Surely it would have been better to have treated the animals close to home, even if the disease was so contagious they would not have been allowed to receive visits from their loved ones.

The sheep and chickens were the worst affected. Intelligence from elsewhere as well as evidence from the research was that the disease was spread by coughing and breathing, so those animals living in close proximity to each other were most at risk. Was there any other reason?

The lockdown was hard on everyone. The animals were bored, miserable and scared. Depression was widespread. Loneliness, lack of exercise, starvation: these were all huge problems, perhaps even more than the illness itself.

Rations were reduced, although the pigs looked as well fed and plump as ever. Food production was down, trade was down, the Farm was getting poorer. Only essential workers kept working. The sheep and llamas were still sheared and their wool taken away for manufacture. The chickens kept laying, but it took time for transport to get started again, so there were many breakages and considerable waste as eggs went bad. The hens could not protect them all until they hatched.

Diego was still working, but he had been uncharacteristically slow and ponderous since his son's death. His wife had recovered from her ordeal. Even though scientists were desperately needed to get them through the pandemic, she could not find work. She confided in Clara and Bella that she forced herself to be strong and positive for the sake of their daughter. She worried about Diego and he struggled even more during the lockdown.

The IHO recommended methods to control and beat the virus; isolating animals showing signs of infection and those that had been in contact with them in one barn, acquiring medical supplies, cleaning all areas regularly, banning movement of animals between farms other than to trade essential supplies and provisions.

Announcements were made by Mickey and his team, but the measures were not properly implemented. He put his daughter's husband in charge of the emergency despite the young pig never having shown himself capable of managing anything. And still the disease spread. Most animals tried hard to maintain social distancing, but a minority argued that it infringed their animal rights, either because they believed the virus was a hoax or because they thought they were too young and healthy to be at risk.

And animals were dying. What was Mickey's response? He blamed the IHO for a failure of leadership and for kowtowing to Mung Farm. The disease had started in Mung and, despite gossip, it was not known exactly why. There was some evidence that the owners had hidden both the existence and the extent of the pandemic until it was widely known and they could hide it no longer. Once they admitted the problem though, the Mungs cooperated fully with the IHO, sharing what their doctors had learned about the illness and how to treat it. Mung was a wealthy and productive farm. It produced food, equipment and medication that Manor Farm needed. Mickey threatened to cease all trade, placing all the blame on 'Mung flu'.

Nelson could contain himself no longer. He issued a statement, which was read out all over the Farm by the dogs and their supporters. Under his Presidency, there had been a well-developed plan to manage serious outbreaks of infectious diseases. Indeed, during his term of office, there had been a serious illness outside which threatened to spread to the Farm. Although only one animal on Manor Farm had died, Mickey had denounced him and demanded his resignation. Nelson's successful pandemic plan had been torn up and thrown away and scientists had lost their jobs. Now Mickey was refusing to pay the Farm's contribution to the IHO. Nelson said this was wrong, dangerous and, whilst it would impact on all, the weakest and those in need would be most affected. As ever, his words were measured and his love for his fellow creatures evident. The dogs and many other animals were moved. More than ever, they missed his intelligence and integrity.

Twenty Six

Mickey's outbursts were getting wilder and more savage. He said Mung Farm had sent the virus deliberately to punish Manor Farm for its success. When questioned about the high death rate, he veered alarmingly between disputing the figures and saying 'It is what it is,' adding that he had been sent from the Sugar Candy Mountain to save the Farm.

The pigeons were exhausted, after long days and nights tweeting his attacks on Jack and Lucia, the Mung and immigrants for plotting against him. Despite the lockdown, Mickey continued to hold barn meetings, claiming that he was mixing with his fellow creatures and that he was working tirelessly to overcome the virus. But Clara noticed that he kept away from all animals, except a few of the pigs closest to him. And he was spotted playing games and entertaining so he could not be working as hard as he claimed.

As the death rate rose, the pig police redoubled their efforts at enforcing the lockdown. Movement around the Farm was severely restricted. Small teams were responsible for cleaning and disinfecting premises and vehicles. Barriers were placed between patches of land

and individual sheds, stables and stalls to try to slow the spread of the disease.

It had been agreed that masks were too hard for animals to put on, uncomfortable and ineffective at properly covering noses, snouts and muzzles. So cleaning and restrictions on movement were critical. Most animals obeyed, but some struggled, especially those species used to having the run of the farm – foxes, rats, mice and cats. The birds flew wherever they liked, especially the tweeting pigeons, but Fussy was content with free movement in the air, as long as they did not land until they reached home. The sheep and especially the lambs did not see why they should be confined to their pastures, even though their death rate was still rising. Mickey was uncharacteristically quiet when he was asked to tell them to keep to the rules.

He was more vocal about the aid package his administration put in place, claiming credit for it, even though most of the ideas came from Lucia. But, whereas her intention was to help the weakest and poorest animals, Mickey's measures supported the owners and managers and he argued that the benefit would trickle down to the animals who worked for them or lived on their land. Some animals still trusted him and believed every pronouncement, but more and more had doubts as their rations were reduced again.

Were the controls stopping the spread of the disease? It seemed they were having some effect, but breaches led to new outbreaks. Fussy's increasingly urgent messages were communicated across the Farm. Every animal knew or had heard of someone who had the illness. The news from other Farms was mixed. The most efficient were controlling it through tough regimes of testing and quarantining while others were less rigorous and the disease was rife.

Clara missed her friends. She was happy when she found a place where she could meet Bella, each in their permitted area, calling out so they could speak to each other.

'Have you heard?' she asked Bella. 'Apparently, we're running out of cleaning materials.'

'I'm sure there will be more arriving soon' Bella said, to herself as much as to Clara. She was sad and confused. Since the dinner party and her discovery that the pigs were eating lamb, she had been scared, so scared that she persuaded Clara to say nothing. She no longer regarded Mickey as a great leader, but she hoped he would do his best to protect the Farm and its residents.

'And there's no room at hospitals on other Farms, because they're full' Clara added.

Bella did not reply. She had heard that too and she knew of cows lying in their sheds, weak, ill, with little or no medication. She missed her friends, her work, her life. She was not clever like Clara, but she watched, listened and thought about what she saw and heard. Nothing gave her confidence that these terrible times would come to an end. Indeed, thinking about the future filled her with dread.

Twenty Seven

Bella's fears proved accurate.

Mickey was interviewed on Rat News. He said that everyone knew cleanliness was crucial to stopping the virus spreading and also that bleach was the best disinfectant. If it killed the virus outside the body, then it followed that it must be able to kill it inside the body too. He asked scientists to investigate this and he boasted that he had come up with the solution.

Most animals laughed when they heard this, the only funny moment they had had since pandemic began. Others were disgusted, both at the stupidity of the suggestion and the risk it posed to those who were gullible enough to take him seriously. Fussy was asked what he thought and he said that bleach was a very dangerous substance and should never ever be ingested. But a small number of the dimmest sheep had complete faith in Mickey as their leader. They drank bleach and died.

Things were even worse for the chickens. Restrictions on their movement even before the Halo Virus, egg quotas and lack of respect for them and their hard work all played on their minds as they had more time to think during the lockdown. The pig police were noticeably rougher with chickens than they were with other species. Matters came to a head when one chicken was stopped for being in possession of grain, which the police thought did not belong to him. He protested that the grain was part of his rations, but they did not believe him. One of the policemen held him down while they waited for reinforcements. By the time they arrived, the chicken was dead.

This death lit a fuse in the chicken community. Under the slogan 'Chicken's Lives Matter,' they marched to the White Barn, joined by many animal supporters who agreed that this was murder and that chickens had been badly treated for too long.

Mickey was furious, blaming the 'chicken coup' for food shortages and denouncing the protestors as 'jerk chicken'.

Lucia, Jack and the dogs sympathised with the chickens. Nelson spoke movingly about understanding their suffering and the need for justice and equal rights. Mickey and his followers condemned criminal behaviour and violence by chickens, even though there was no evidence of this. They squealed, bleated and tweeted loudly that 'All Animals Lives Matter', but they were in a minority.

'Of course, all animal lives matter' Clara told Bella. 'But it's chickens who suffer most, so we must support them'. She was thrilled when Bella said she agreed. For the first time since the Revolution, it seemed that there was an opportunity for real change, if only the Farm could return to normal after the virus.

Twenty Eight

The virus and the lockdown brought with them dangers other than the illness itself. When times were difficult, rations tight and animals fearing for their lives and futures, it was easy to sow the seeds of division. Chickens suffered most, but donkeys had problems too.

The immediate issue was a donkey sanctuary on a plot close to the border. On many farms, donkeys were forced to work hard, carry heavy loads and some were beaten and even killed by their human owners. Years ago, after prolonged and terrible suffering on one farm, they were provided with a sanctuary on a site where many of their ancestors had once lived and where a small number of donkeys still lived. It was a place where the older beasts could rest and recuperate. Younger donkeys joined them and soon there were families.

The problem was that the fields had been home to rabbits many of whom ran away when the donkeys arrived. Some donkeys wanted to live in peace with the rabbits. Others were less friendly, because they feared rabbit diseases and rabbits eating their crops. Similarly, some rabbits wanted to share the site with donkeys, but others did everything they could to hurt the settlers. The rabbits remaining on the sanctuary were badly treated and those who had left were agitating to come back. This was a hard problem to solve, because there was right and wrong on both sides. Previous leaders had tried to broker agreements without success.

Mickey claimed to have a peace plan, but he had no understanding of the context, the complexity of the situation or of how to make change happen. He only succeeded in worsening the tensions between the rabbits and the donkeys.

Clara loved all animals. She explained to Bella and Diego. 'All animals are my brothers and sisters. I'm so lucky to be living on Manor Farm even when it's run by Mickey, but I know how different donkeys' lives are on other farms. It breaks my heart to see how the rabbits live in the sanctuary.' She hoped that Jack would win the election and he would broker a solution so the two species could live together in peace.

But the sanctuary was not the only problem. Stories circulated about donkeys being disloyal to Manor and secretly running all farms everywhere. Was it because their memories were so good? There were wealthy donkeys, but they were a small minority and no different to any other rich animals. Clara knew many poor and stupid donkeys, so there was no reason for this prejudice. In normal times, only a few animals thought this way, but with the pressure of lockdown and Mickey's leadership, the atmosphere was tense. From her reading of history, she knew that bad feelings against chickens and donkeys increased during difficult times and that made her afraid. The weakest animals needed someone to blame.

The conspiracy theories became more outlandish and they were spreading. Although only a minority was taken in, she feared that the more often they were repeated, the more animals would be convinced. The theories centred on a donkey that had escaped from captivity as a youth and become rich and successful. The pig supremacists objected to a donkey having more than they did. And they were horrified when he used his wealth to help poor and disadvantaged animals whether they were on the Farm or elsewhere. Rumours spread that the virus was a plot by him and his allies to take control of the Farm, which he would do by implanting a microchip in the vaccine. Clara was devastated by how many animals believed it. The more sensible animals ignored the scare stories, but their voices were in danger of being drowned out. Mickey did not say he agreed, but he described pig supremacists as 'fine people' and the pigeons denounced the rich donkey. She feared for her species if this hatred was not stopped and for all the animals if vaccine refusal resulted in a longer pandemic with more loss of life.

Twenty Nine

Mickey had never wanted to lock down. His followers protested against the restrictions, claiming it was against their animal rights to stop them doing what they wanted to do. They marched between plots, ignoring social distancing, risking their lives and those of their fellow creatures. They shared a common belief that their lives should not be restricted. Their reasons varied – some thought the virus did not exist and was fake news, some that it was an evil plot to control the population and others that they would not catch it. Mickey looked to be panicking, because he understood that elections were won and lost on how prosperous the voters felt themselves to be. The sooner he could get everybody back working, the more likely it was he would win. So he started to relax the lockdown and promised it would be completely lifted soon. His supporters were delighted, chanting his name and goading the dogs.

Fussy warned that it was much too soon to reopen the Farm and that lives would be lost unnecessarily. Mickey simply said he was wrong and intimated that his advice had been faulty throughout the pandemic. Fussy and his family needed police protection due to threats of violence. Mickey did not condone this, but nor

did he condemn it. Perhaps he had lost control.
Perhaps he did not care.

His attacks on Jack, who was known to be a
good dog and a safe pair of paws, were
increasingly frenzied. Repeating the Slack Jack
and Cracked Jack sneers, he denounced his
opponent as old and feeble minded. It was true
that Jack was old, but only a little older than
Mickey himself and he always sounded articulate
and sensible when he spoke. By contrast,
Mickey's pronouncements were becoming more
troubling. In public, he seemed to have some
difficulty pronouncing names and words, even
simple ones like the names of other farms. And
he did not just stumble with words. His gait was
awkward and he always had a pig aide with him
to help him walk. He countered, saying 'Vets
cannot believe how healthy I am. I'm the
healthiest president in the history of the Farm
ever. Don't believe the lies of the evil dogs.'

Clara despaired of the times they were living in.
History had taught her that good days would
eventually follow bad days, provided the Halo
Virus could be contained or destroyed. How
long that would take she dared not guess. The
mood was changing, but slowly. Only the
dimmest Mickey supporters continued to put
their faith in their leader. They were still a
substantial force on the Farm and they
expressed their views aggressively, but their

numbers were dwindling. Would that be enough to defeat Mickey?

She spoke to everyone she knew, trying to persuade them of the importance of voting for Jack.

Diego had not recovered his vigour and optimism. He would never be the same after the loss of his son. But his wife had persuaded him to get on with life and make the best of it for their own sakes and that of their daughter. They were living in Manor Farm, he had work, they had a nice stall and reasonable rations. The lockdown had given him time to think and he came out of it a calmer llama with a new sense of perspective. He began to work harder again, for the good of the Farm and his fellow creatures. As for voting, he would leave politics to those who understood better than him.

Bella was uncertain. She would never forget watching the pigs eating lamb. She was worried by the strange things Mickey said and wondered whether he was ill. Two things finally convinced her. Firstly, the most sensible and honourable pigs turned against him. A group called Cadillac issued statements and placed advertisements on the radio criticising Mickey. Disgusted with what they described as his incompetence and corruption, they argued that he was not fit to be leader. They urged all animals to ignore their species loyalty and to vote for Jack, a good dog, who had shown his dedication to the Farm over many years. 'Back Jack' was trending all over the Farm. Secondly, she listened to Jack. He was gentle, calm and he had worked very closely with Nelson. Bella realised she liked him. She did not like Mickey. And once she had made up her mind, it all became clear. She resented the idea that she had been fooled by Mickey. She decided she would vote for Jack.

Thirty

Fussy was proved right. The virus continued to spread and more animals died. Campaigning for the election continued, mainly through radio, tweets and word of mouth. Jack was careful because of Halo, but Mickey continued to hold rallies.

Lucia defended Jack against vicious attacks, countering the jibes with the highly effective 'Back Jack' campaign. But she knew that Mickey's base was strong and she understood and feared his strategy.

Firstly, he wanted chaos and disorder so he could claim to be a strong and decisive leader, the only one who could control the Farm. Jack would be painted as weak

For that, he needed enemies both internal and external.

Internally, the pig police were still treating the chickens badly and the death of another young chicken led to protests by chickens and the animals who shared their pain. There were battles in the fields with crops destroyed. No one knew whether this was caused by genuine anger at chicken's suffering or deliberate provocation by extremists either for or against Mickey. It frightened the ordinary animals who just wanted a calm and happy farm. Jack condemned violence, but he supported the right to protest peacefully against injustice. It was a difficult balance to strike. Mickey's simplistic message of restoring order was simpler to understand.

Externally, Mung Farm was Mickey's main enemy, held responsible for both the 'Mung Flu' pandemic and unfair trade, which he blamed for the suffering and restrictions on the Farm. As the election approached, his anti Mung rhetoric became wilder. 'Just how far would he go?' Lucia asked herself. Would he start a battle with Mung, sacrificing more lives so he could be re-elected? She thought he would if he thought it would work. He had no limits.

Secondly, there was the integrity and fairness of the election itself.

She had no doubt that Ivan and the Soys would meddle again. It suited them for Mickey to remain President. No one knew why he seemed to do as Ivan wanted. Did the Soy leader have power over him? And what would they do this time round to make sure their pig remained in power?

Elections had always been tightly managed so they were free and fair, but Mickey's henchpigs were in all the key positions and they were making changes which would boost his chances. Funding for the team that checked only Farm residents voted was cut, which would make it easier for fraudulent voting. And the number and locations of polling stations were changed. Dogs, goats and chickens would all have to travel across the Farm through areas where the virus was rife, a risk some might not be prepared to take. By contrast, pigs and sheep had several places to vote in or close to where they lived.

Even though it was his pig allies who were organising the election with arrangements designed to favour him, Mickey complained that the dogs were cheating. He realised support for his presidency was dropping. His fragile ego would not be able to cope with rejection. He even intimated that he might not accept the result if he lost. The owls were already busy considering Lucia and the dogs' challenges to the new election arrangements. If Jack won and he refused to step down, they would be working full time on his objections and Jack's demand for the presidency. The chaos did not bear thinking about. Democracy and the rule of law were at stake.

Thirty One

One evening, Bella met Clara properly for the first time since the lockdown. Clara was delighted to see her cow friend was wearing a 'Back Jack' cap. Even the horrifying prospect of Mickey remaining president was not enough to spoil their enjoyment. They chatted happily and made plans to meet again the next day to decide what they could do to support Jack and the dogs.

As they said goodbye, Bella turned to go back to her stall. The walk was not a long one, but she started to feel a little dizzy. 'It must be the excitement' she told herself. 'I'll be fine tomorrow.' But as the night wore on, she felt worse and worse. She slept fitfully and by morning she was a sick cow. Coughing, weakness, fatigue, aching muscles, Bella had the virus. She was quarantined, unable to see anyone or even to get a message to Clara.

Days passed. She hoped she had not passed the virus to Clara. She prayed she would be one of the lucky ones, with a mild case from which she would recover quickly with no long term damage. But she found it hard to breathe and the pain was unbearable. Unable to move, she was seriously ill. A vet was called. He examined her carefully, taking her temperature, checking her pulse and listening to her breathing. He shook his head. 'I'm afraid there's no choice. You have to go to hospital.'

Bella was terrified. She had never left the Farm before. Everyone had heard stories of animals who had gone to hospitals on other farms and very few returned. Too weak to walk, she was carried to a van and put to lie down in the back. As they drove through the farm towards the entrance gate, she could just see out of the back window. She watched as the fields, meadows and homes of her beloved Farm disappeared into the distance.

Word about her plight must have reached Clara and Diego. She glimpsed them, waiting anxiously at the gate. Just as the driver was about to take them through, Clara threw herself at the van and Bella heard her call out 'Stay strong. You'll get through this. You'll be back here before you know it. We love you.'

Bella was too feeble to call back, too feeble even to lift her head. Tears rolled down her face, devastated that she had not even been able to say goodbye to her friends. As they drove on, across unfamiliar land to a strange and frightening place, she thought about the Farm – the beautiful and prosperous land and the love and fellowship of animals, now facing the combined threats of a terrible virus, hatred, violence and misrule. Would she survive the virus? Would she ever see Manor Farm again? Would the nightmare of the Mickey era ever end? And, if she lived and she made it back, would it still be the Farm she knew and loved?

ACKNOWLEDGEMENTS

This story was born of the boredom and frustration of lockdown. As the best politicians, organisations and scientists struggle to defeat Covid-19, the deficiencies of too many governments have been exposed. Economic shock leads almost inevitably to political and social change. Extremism and racism were already rising with the Far Right emboldened and dangers on the Left too. The threats to democracy are evident and there are few measured, effective and compassionate leaders just when they are most needed.

'May you live in interesting times' may or may not be a real Chinese curse. Now I live in interesting times and I wish I did not. So this is my howl of anger. I hope it strikes a chord. I am, of course, no George Orwell. I pay homage to him.

My main source of information is the much maligned mainstream media. Everything else, good and bad, is mine.

I have people to thank. Danni Henning has produced a brilliant cover. She has a great future ahead of her. Most importantly, I thank my friends and family, especially my late husband Martin (who I miss every day and who should have been with me through the lockdown) and our daughter Rebecca. I must also mention the few people who knew I was writing and who encouraged me. And finally thank you to all those people, public and private, whose actions, behaviours and attitudes provoked me so much I had to write a book.